Hippity Hoppity

Ho Ho Ho

Written by Kelly Wilkins

Illustrated by Danh Tran

Edited by Cheri Jackson

To: Zachary & William,
Be careful what you wish for !
Warm Wishes,
Kelly Wilkins

Dedication

This book is dedicated with love to my Bug and Lil Monkey, Brantley & Brecklyn.

Without you, Hippity Hoppity would not be. To Vic and Jessa for #5. And to my wife Ashli for her continued support and love throughout the writing of this book. Love you all to the moon and back!

Reading is knowledge

Knowledge is power

Power is strength

Strength is to know that the more you read

The stronger you will grow

Love,

Mama

It was a very long winter and a very tough year.
Santa needed a vacation, somewhere warm and not very near.

He gathered his belongings and kissed Mrs. Claus goodbye.
She knew Santa would be gone for a while and let out with a sigh.

He flew off quickly with warm weather in sight.
He knew everything at the North Pole would be all right.

He found a place with warm tropical sun,
jumped out of his sleigh and began to run.

He placed his chair by the salty sea.
Santa knew this was the place to be.

Suddenly, he heard a ruckus and turned just slight.
He thought, *Wow! It's the Easter Bunny. Why is he uptight?*

Santa called out, "Hey Bunny! What is with all the clatter?
What is going on over there? What is the matter?"

The Easter Bunny started grumbling and jumping all around,
"The eggs are not even close to being done to deliver all over town!"

"All night long down the bunny trail, I hip and I hop along,
 delivering eggs and baskets to everyone. I cannot get it wrong!"

"That is nothing." said good Old Saint Nick.
"You try squeezing down chimneys quietly. I must use every trick!"

They both thought for a moment,
What would it be like to change roles for a season?
Do they have to tell everyone and give them a reason?

Bunny shrieked with excitement,
"Let's make a wish and try it, all right?
Let's wish upon a star. Let's do it tonight!"

Night was approaching and they both did agree
to change roles for a season, just so they could see.

As the first star shined that they saw in their sight,
they said these magical words to make the wish just right.

"Star light, star bright, the first star we see tonight,
we wish we may, we wish we might, have this wish we wish tonight."

And as they continued to spout,
they said what their wish was truly about.

"Hippity, Hoppity, Ho, Ho, Ho!
Let us change roles.
Now here we go!"

Soon, right after, to their big surprise,
their physical appearances changed right before their eyes!

"Wow, look at us! We did it Bunny!"
Santa proclaimed as he gave his new ears a pinch.
"Now I will do Easter. This will be a cinch!"

Spring was finally here and the eggs were all done.
Santa gathered every basket, one by one.

Off he went hopping, all around town.
Soon his feet started to hurt. He needed to sit down.

He began to throw eggs! He began to show a frown.
He was making such a mess. He was making too much sound!

"This is hard work, I do so agree.
I understand now what Bunny was saying to me."

No sooner did Christmas come around and it was Bunny's turn to try.
The elves loaded up his sleigh and he was ready to go fly.

The reindeer flew very fast, up and over every hill.
Bunny hollered with excitement, "This is very scary, but also a fun thrill!"

He landed on the first house and it was very slick!
He knew he had to hurry. He knew he must be quick!

Heading to the chimney, almost forgetting all his toys,
he wiggled on down as he sucked in his belly, making a very loud noise.

Reaching the bottom, all covered in soot, Bunny groaned, "Santa lied! I did not land on my feet like he said. I landed on my side!"

"Also, this bag is so heavy!" as he threw the presents under the tree. "I understand why Santa is so tough. Now I can see."

Peering over his shoulder, just to his right,
was a plate full of cookies Bunny could see in his sight.

He tried to resist them, but ate in such a hurry,
then dashed over to the chimney in a fast, fast fury.

Moaning as he inched his way up, little by little.
"Wow! I should not have eaten that last cookie.
I'm so big around my middle."

Reaching the top, breathless and gasping,
"This is hard work, I do so agree.
I understand now what Santa was saying to me."

Well, the holidays came and went. It was time to relax.
"Santa, it is time to go on vacation." Bunny sent via fax.

They both met again in the warm tropical sun.
Santa's belly shook as he asked, "Did you think it was fun?"

Bunny cried, "The tricks did not help me like you had said!
I fell down the chimney sideways and even bumped my head!"

Santa replied, "Well, you did not tell me that my feet would be so sore
and that I would have to keep hopping and delivering more and more!"

Both their jobs were hard, they did agree.
They did not need to stay switched, for no reason they could see.

So that night, as the first star shined that they saw in their sight,
they once again said the magical words to make it just right.

"Star light, star bright, the first star we see tonight.
We wish we may, we wish we might, have this wish we wish tonight."

And as they continued to spout,
they said what their wish was truly about.

"Hippity, Hoppity, Ho, Ho, Ho!
Let us change roles.
Now here we go!"

This time it was to no surprise
when they changed back to their original selves before their own eyes.

Santa's ears shrank and Bunny's belly was gone!
They were back to themselves. It did not take long.

They jumped for joy! They both were excited.
They gave high fives. They were very delighted!

So now you heard the tale of when Santa and Bunny changed for a season,
to see if their lives would be better for no apparent reason.

Therefore, next time you look into the night sky and see a bright light afar,
be careful what you wish for, when wishing upon a star.

CPSIA information can be obtained
at www.ICGtesting.com
Printed in the USA
BVOW05s1932300917
496350BV00003B/7/P

9 780998 649900